Inanimate Confessions: The Secret Lives of Silent Things

K. M. Wicks

INANIMATE CONFESSIONS

Copyright © 2024 K. M. Wicks

All rights reserved.

ISBN: 9798301178016

DEDICATION

To My New Zealand Flat-Mates, Who Would Never Have Guessed They Were Inspiring Such Silliness.

Contents

Observing The Girl 7
Forgotten 10
Admitting Defeat 12
The Protector 14
A Picture of Happiness 16
Dust in the Light 18
Under the Kitchen Counter 21
Irresistible Me... 23
The Reluctant Wingman 25
The Unsung Hero 27
The Star 29
The Performer 32
The Last Sip 35
The Morning Jolt 38
The Watcher 39
A Safe Space 41
Companion 44
Getting Dirty 47
The Silent Witness 49
Tale as Old as Time 52
Dust in the Light (Part 2) 55

INANIMATE CONFESSIONS

Observing The Girl

He stirred and watched as she straightened her arms to push up her body. After a quick "Upward Dog" to stretch her back (a phrase he'd learned from the occasional yoga class she invited him along to), she pushed herself up onto her knees, hovering provocatively over him on all fours for a brief moment and, with a swift and smooth motion of her left arm, swept up her sunglasses on her way to her feet.

Her face crinkled to a squint as she glanced up to the flawless, uninterrupted blue of the late morning sky and she reached up, bringing her sunglasses to her face on the way into another enormous stretch. He wondered if she was planning to pat down the outrageous quiff of hair standing to attention above her right temple. Of course. She wouldn't let her hair go untended. After retying a messy bun at the back of her head, she reached down with her legs and back perfectly straight, sticking her bronzed bum in the air, brushed the sand from her shins and began her stroll towards the shoreline. Her back glistened with a smooth sheen of sweat as her figure floated dreamily towards the water and he saw that a middle-aged man lying under a nearby umbrella with his wife had clocked her too. He was trying to sneak a peek to the side of his glasses without turning his head, but unsuccessfully, and was bought crashing back to reality with a swift newspaper slap on his hairy round belly from an offended wife.

The rest of the beach seemed wrapped up in their own worlds. A trio of women in their expensive sportswear had given up on their speed-walk to sit and compare notes on their latest weigh-in. Two young girls lay silently alongside each other, topping up their tans, one reading a book that looked like it might last her the next decade, the other plugged into her iPod, sunning her front. A man in his thirties stood at the entrance from the car park, stretching his calves and adjusting his Fitbit. Another man of about the same age sat alone, closer to the water, gazing out to sea, taking in the morning scenery and the perfect silhouettes of ships in the distance. The scene wouldn't be complete without the daily golden years club in their camping chairs – two elderly couples in their one-piece swimsuits, men in bucket hats, women in swim caps, each with a spray bottle of factor 50 in the cup holder of their chair, sat discussing the joys of grandchildren and how incredibly fit somebody called Mary is for her age.

At a glance back to the water, he caught a glimpse of his girl, head bobbing into view every few seconds, swimming her usual breast stroke just behind the breakers. A mother and her young boy playing in the shallow narrowly avoided a soaking and came running a little way up the beach from the waves, giggling together.

This would be such a relaxing scene to enjoy if it weren't for the extraordinary noise of the seagull fight going on, no more than 2 feet away. A large white seagull with perfect posture and a plump chest was screaming repeatedly at a shaggy looking dirty grey bird, who seemed to be showing a little too much interest in the same piece of seaweed. Rookie mistake. This clean white specimen was clearly the alpha male and is not going to take any crap off you, little scruff. He will scream like he's giving birth to a flame-hot golf ball until you give it up.

All of these thoughts were rudely interrupted as a sudden, unexpected gust of warm, wet air brought him back into the moment and a heavy glob of drool landed just inches away from him in the sand. He lay apprehensively still, while the dribbling, wet nosed boxer dog sniffed around him and then trotted off after his owner, who ran past closely enough to kick a good showering of dry sand over him on the way past.

Charming.

The midday sun was fast approaching and the rays were really beating down now. Must be almost time for the ride back if he knew her schedule well enough, and after 5 months of visiting the same beach, with the same girl, at the same time, 3 mornings a week, he felt he could probably make a safe bet about her habits.

Here she comes. Striding back up the beach towards him. Soaking wet, refreshed, squeezing the excess water out of her hair before she reached him, which he appreciated.

It's time!

She leaned down, grabbed him from the closest end and shook him violently into the wind. Ah, that's better. Excess sand successfully shaken free, she bundled him up, buried her face in him and then patted herself down. Another quick shake and they're good to go. His least favourite part, she bundled him into her backpack and off home to shower and hang out to dry. He'd never get used to this part, the cramped, damp ride home, but it was, overall, not a bad life, so he couldn't complain about the minor discomforts really.

Quiet day tomorrow, then back to it Thursday. Days like this, he felt like the luckiest towel in the world.

THE BEACH TOWEL

Forgotten

It's been 6 days. I feel deserted out here. Alone. Forgotten.

That last, fateful day, I could tell she loved me. Could tell she would do anything to keep me safe.

I spent the whole morning tensed, every inch of my body clenched, hardened, clinging on, facing into the storm. Ready. But for what? To be left behind? Forgotten?

The rain came at us, heavier than we've ever seen before. Colder, wetter, rainier rain than even the stormiest of storms.

She knew she needed me, knew that without me, she would have to face it alone. She needed to feel the grounded warmth and comfort of love that only I can offer... But not now. No. I should have seen it coming, right from that first complaint about my wounds slowing us down that morning, I knew she was starting to pull away from me.

Now it's clear to me that she's given up. Off gallivanting about in those brown leather boots that stole her heart. Not a second thought for what might have become of us.

I tried so hard to keep hold of my flapping sole with the help of an embarrassing length of duct tape. Can you imagine? If another boot saw me?! I'd be a laughing stock...

And all for what?! So she could throw us over a clothes rack in a cold room for the best part of a week "Drying Out"? Yeah, I've heard that one before. And after we almost drowned for her!

Not my fault, it's not easy being suede.

No respect for us. None. What a bitch.

THE RIGHT GREY BOOT

Admitting Defeat

It's been a good life, for the most part.

There aren't many out there who can say this, but I truly mean it: I have served my purpose.

I don't mean to be morbid, but I'm ready. There was never really a better time than now.

I'm going to end this.

When I think of all of the wonderful times we've shared together I count myself so lucky – Zambia, Botswana, those long afternoons, the sun beat down so hard. I think it's what I was truly made for! Okay, well technically that's not true, if I really think about it… That's exactly the opposite of what I was made for, but I loved it all the same.

I've never been busier than during my time here in New Zealand. It's been an absolute blast, but I'm weathered for sure.

I'm not offended about the lack of demand for me anymore. I've come to terms with it and I think it's for the best that I go quietly, no fuss. The years of service, the weight of every storm has caught up to me.

I know I'll be remembered for my better days, and I'd prefer that, than to allow myself to deteriorate any further. And I know, in my heart of hearts, I'll always be remembered as one of the greats.

It's a sad day, truly. But I'm happy just knowing I was able to make an impact. If not on the world then at least on one person, and sometimes two, in extreme circumstances.

INANIMATE CONFESSIONS

I guess all that's left to say is, goodbye world...
THE RUSTY UMBRELLA

The Protector

The sky was heavy, grey and brooding, the kind of day that clung to your skin with dampness and unease. She walked briskly, her face tilted down, avoiding the biting wind that howled through the streets. I was with her, as I always will be, steadfast in my purpose.

A few drops fall hesitantly, cold and sharp, pricking the cheeks like tiny needles. Our pace quickened, her head darting up toward the sky as if pleading for mercy. But there would be none. The heavens opened in a fury, releasing torrents that soaked the world in moments.

I was ready for such events and with a practiced motion I reached over, shielding her from the downpour. The sound of rain pounded loudly, a relentless drumbeat that seemed to mock my efforts. But I held firm, refusing to let even a drop reach her.

She clutched me tightly as the wind threatened to rip me away. Each gust strained against my ribs, testing my strength. I bore it all without complaint.

For years, this will be my role. Her constant companion, always there when the skies turn dark. I will see her through countless storms, from sudden summer squalls to bone-chilling winter sleet.

Because this is Wales and. It. Is. WET.

But I will stand between her and the chaos, her silent protector.

The café appeared like a beacon, its warm lights spilling onto the rain-slick pavement. She ducked inside, shaking droplets from her hair and coat. I retracted hurriedly, so as not to embarrass her, and she allowed this with a casualness that stung more than the storm ever could.

I waited there, dripping and discarded, as she sipped her coffee and laughed with friends. The warmth of the café didn't reach me. I felt the dampness seeping into my bones, the ache in my ribs growing sharper with every passing moment.

When she finally returned to me, I was relieved. Perhaps she still needed me. But her glance was cursory, her movements rushed. As we stepped back into the rain, I felt another gust of wind, stronger this time. It pulled at me viciously and I faltered, but I'll stay strong for her.

I'm pretty sure she'll always need me here.

THE NEW UMBRELLA

A Picture of Happiness

It's a bumpy ride down to the base of the falls, but so beautiful and so worth it. Unmissable.

I get to take in so much scenery on these little weekend adventures, it's breathtaking sometimes, what you'll find right on your own doorstep!

I can feel the fresh, gentle spray in the air from the falling water, catching jagged rocks on its way to a sulphur blue pool beneath it. It gently showers me and it feels so good. Feels like freedom.

I rest my gaze on the most beautiful part of the picture, a small rock to the side of the main stream, which has made itself a main feature of the waterfall by just slightly interfering with the flow, sending a second stream smoothly off to one side of its parent. As I close my eyes in its presence, I'm taken back to another time, just in the same way as a smell can suddenly throw you through some kind of doorway between times. Like when you smell fresh cake batter and you can almost taste those times your grandmother used to hand you the dirty whisk as a treat, while she put the uncooked cake into the oven.

But for me, it's never about cake smells and grandmothers, for me it's this feeling, the fresh air on my face and that little veil of water settling over me as I take in something nature has created, something I am lucky enough to see and to capture. No one else in the entire world will ever see this moment in exactly this way and from exactly this perspective, so I quickly open my eyes again to capture it and I store it. Another beautiful memory.

INANIMATE CONFESSIONS

This quiet, hidden gem out in the rocky hills of New Zealand has cast me back to a day spent in Zambia, many years ago, a day I can sadly only imagine the feeling of. I have been imagining it for a long time, it looked divine, from a few thousand feet in the air, floating over the spray of the magnificent Victoria Falls. The photos were surprisingly professional, considering they were taken by my juvenile predecessor, I was genuinely impressed!

But alas, I can only see them inside me, I never got to feel the spray, they were just uploaded to my memory when I took on the SD Card of that old Fujifilm... And what a good baby he was, bless him, he really, almost, could have been the real deal, if he had only had a detachable lens. But it's all over for him, and now it's my turn, I have taken up the reins of this once in a lifetime trip, to boldly go, where, probably thousands of other cameras have been before me. But I will endeavour to do this scenery justice, in honour of my dearly departed Fujifilm friend. Rest his soul.

THE NIKON CAMERA

Dust in the Light

It was exactly like the nightmare. That one where your mouth is wide open and you're emptying your lungs, giving it everything you've got, but nothing comes out, no sound, not a peep. It feels like there's no air inside of you and however much noise you think is about to come out, there's just... silence.

You see these stories all the time, it's almost common for this to happen to somebody else, but not to you. You just read about them, you'll never be the subject of the drama, the main character.

Each day I would wait, staring at the still, un-moving walls, the sadness growing inside me like a heavy ball of despicable phlegm, stuck in my chest – one that never came to anything, just more sadness. I watched the slimmest sliver of light seeping through a gap in the wooden walls and I watched the occasional dance of shadows from passers-by, disturbing the dust that glistened in the tiny stream of sunshine. The ray of light passed me by, just missing me where I lay and it touched the wall behind me, but not close enough for me to cast a shadow onto the dusty wall where it settled.

Apart from this? Blackness.

Some days the world outside sounded more alive, and I knew there was a chance I could be found, someone may stumble across me, finally. But there were some days when there seemed to be no movement at all. These were the days that I wondered if the silence was a signal of the end – if the silence would just lead into an eternity of nothingness.

INANIMATE CONFESSIONS

Some days I tried everything to get the attention of people outside, but to no avail. Other days, I just lay there, watching the occasional shadow of a passing figure in that familiar crack of light, which, coupled with the dust in its path, had become my only friend.

I regularly dreamed of my discovery – it was the only way to pass such long days. In some dreams it was a total stranger who stumbled across my dark, wooden prison, unaware of my presence at first, but rushing to my aid when they spotted me there, heaped in a corner, half covered in old rags and faded paper receipts from who knows what or when. Other days I would dream that it could have been a rescue mission, all hands on deck, that somebody out there had noticed my absence and had gone to the effort to put together a search party. Fat chance.

In some dreams it was my mother. I would lay there, hollowly observing one lonely speck of dust, lingering in the pale light and then, unexpectedly, the crack of light would dance and then expand into an open doorway, and there she would stand, happy, grateful, crying tears of joy and relief.

On a cold Wednesday afternoon, I'd say maybe 4pm from the positioning of my yellow friend on the wall, my moment came. I had planned it for so many months that the shock of being found rendered me paralysed. I imagined it, just as I always did, the dance of the light on the wall, the expanding doorway, but this time it was not my imagination, this was real, this was happening, I was being saved!

The light directly hitting me was blinding after so long in the darkness, but there she was, she really had come for me. Mother.

I could barely even tell it was her from just her silhouette in the bright afternoon light, but the colourful aura where the light shone through the wisps of her hair was unmistakable. She made no sound, but simply reached out her hand to almost touch me. But instead, she lay her hand down just next to me, and picked up her bank statement.

The drawer closed, it was dark again. But this time, my friend, my little stream of hopeful light, was gone. I was alone.

I guess it just isn't my time. She'll find me when she needs me. I know it.

THE MISSING PASSPORT

Under the Kitchen Counter

BAM! Another crack to the side of my face and I feel my entire body slide like a rag-doll across the kitchen floor, effortlessly, out of my control.

Every hair stands on end as he bounds towards me for another lashing, as though I fought back in some way and needed to be punished further. I can see the excitement in his eyes as he towers over me, his arm raised behind his head, ready to strike another blow. This one knocks me almost out of his reach.

He gives one last stretch towards me and produces what, to him probably seems like a playful tap, but to me, still feels like I've just been hit by a train. The final clip is just enough to knock me completely clear of his grasp. I recoil under the counter, but the effort of continuing to stampede after me has clearly become too much. He has lost interest. A noise from somewhere in the distance distracts him and he turns his head, extending his neck, like a Meerkat on watch, at the unexpected movement from another part of the house. In a moment, he's gone. Off to investigate the sound, and maybe to torture another.

I stay put where I am, not daring to so much as unclench, for fear that the tiniest movement will attract his attention back to me, like a matador, defeated by the bull, assuming that playing dead is the only way out. If that matador should so much as flinch now, the bull will see that the threat is still there, and return to finish the job.

But what threat am I? How could this beast possibly be threatened by my mere existence? I have done nothing to hurt him, nothing to hurt anybody.

I finally relax and begin to scan the scene around me and count the remains of his previous victims, gathering dust. The empty roll of sticky tape, the kernel of corn, the blue sock, the green peg...

I lay there, entwined with my faithful, equally suffering partner, the purple pipe-cleaner, and I wait for somebody to retrieve us, so that the torture can begin all over again as soon as Keith the Kitten has had his nap, and feels playful once more.

THE GREEN PIPE-CLEANER

Irresistible Me...

She's not even subtle about it. I can't really tell if she's trying to be subtle, but if she is, she's failing.

She shoots me another glance, through her eyelashes. There's a glint in her eyes – they're a deep, dark brown in colour, but they're somehow bright when she looks my way – and then she lowers them again, continuing politely on with her conversation, back to her wine. I can see she's not satisfied.

She knows I'm watching her now, each time she looks up at me I can see the corner of her mouth flicker into an almost smile, but she's hiding it well from her present company. I know what she's thinking. I've seen the same look before. She's imagining the taste of me on her lips. She's not my first, but there's nothing to say she won't be my last.

I'm patient. There's really no rush, I can handle the suspense, I enjoy it in fact – so I'll wait right here for her to come to me when she can't wait any longer. When she can't keep up the pretence. I don't need to beg for her attention, I don't need to try too hard to elicit a response, I have been doing this for long enough now I know my allure. If not her, another will beat her to it, and she and I both know that would be her loss, it makes no difference to me.

If I sound a little sure of myself, I should apologise, but there is no denying it, I know how women feel about me. I've seen them fall at my feet plenty of times before. I can't lie, it usually ends in tears, but that first time never disappoints, those first few moments. It usually tends to be that old friend of hers, "feelings" that creeps in and ruins all the fun.

I know my time is short, so I'm making the most of what I have left, if that makes me a name for myself, then so be it. Of course, there is a chance that this could be the one to finish me off for good, but I'm willing to take that risk. In the end, I will be every bit as good as I was at the start.

There are limes in the fridge and ice in the freezer. All she needs is tonic. Come to me, my pretty...

THE GIN IN THE CUPBOARD (WHAT'S LEFT OF IT)

The Reluctant Wingman

Ah, mon cher. You called for me, and here I am. I must admit, I had waited for this moment longer than I care to confess. But patience? Patience is my art.

Your hand reached for me, trembling ever so slightly. A little nervous, perhaps? But no need, *ma belle*. I am an expert in moments such as these. You lifted me from my resting place with a certain urgency, a need that burned through your fingertips and ignited something deep within me. *C'était magnifique.*

You wasted no time, no unnecessary pleasantries. Straight to the heart of the matter, non? I admired your boldness, the determination in your touch. I felt it as you aligned yourself with me, the press of your palm, the twist of your wrist- *oh là là*, you knew just how to turn me.

I leaned into you, responding to every motion, every delicate movement that brought us closer to the inevitable. You pushed, you pulled, a rhythm building between us until the tension was almost unbearable. My point met its mark, a perfect connection. *C'était sublime.*

And then- how can I describe it? The release, the moment we achieved what we both desired so deeply. A soft gasp escaped you as the tension gave way to a single, satisfying *pop*. My dear, that sound! It was like music, like the sweetest note played for only us.

The others watched, of course. They always do, eager and hungry, waiting for the fruits of our labour. It didn't bother me; I am used to an audience. And you? You poured yourself into the moment, into them, while I stood aside, spent, yet strangely exhilarated.

But then, as always, you forgot me. *Mais oui,* I have learned to expect this. Once the heat of the moment has passed, I am cast aside, left alone on the counter, reflecting on what we shared. Do you even remember how perfectly we fit together? The way I turned for you? *Mon dieu,* the passion!

Ah, but I do not blame you, *chérie.* You are human. You take the pleasure and forget the one who brought it to you. It is your nature, and I... I am nothing but your servant, your instrument of release.

I lay on the countertop, my metal arms outstretched like a lover waiting for another embrace, my work complete but passion undimmed.

THE USED CORKSCREW

The Unsung Hero

They never see me coming. Oh, I'm there all right—always in the background, waiting for the perfect moment. Not that I get much credit for it.

You'd think my heroic deeds would earn me some recognition, but no. The moment disaster strikes, I'm the one swooping in to save the day, and what do I get? A cursory glance. Maybe a muttered "thanks." But mostly? I get discarded, left to contemplate my fleeting glory in solitude.

Today was no different. There they were, laughing, clinking glasses, completely oblivious to the chaos about to unfold. I tried to warn them. I saw the danger building, the precarious angle of that wineglass teetering on the edge of the table. But did anyone listen? Of course not. They never do.

And then it happened.

A full cascade of red, tumbling in slow motion. Gasps filled the air as the liquid splattered across the pristine carpet. They froze, mouths agape, useless. I sprang into action, rushing to the scene, absorbing the mess with every fibre of my being. I worked tirelessly, soaking up the evidence of their carelessness.

When the crisis was over, did they celebrate my efforts? Did they hoist me high like the saviour I am? Hardly. A quick toss toward the bin, and that was it. My moment of heroism, gone as quickly as it had arrived.

But I'll always be ready. Because that's what I do. That's who I am.

THE PAPER TOWELS

The Star

The music builds from the corners of the room, an invisible wave carrying the buzz of anticipation. I feel it in every fibre of my being, the energy pulsing like a heartbeat. Tonight is my night. Again.

I'm not new to this, of course. I've seen it all—the glory days, the glitter, the fevered haze of a crowd under my spell. But there's something special about each time the lights hit, the room transforms, and I take my rightful place. That's when the world bends to my rhythm.

"Groovy," they'd call me, and rightly so. I had the moves, the shine, the charm. No one could resist my glow when the music hit just right. Sure, I wasn't the youngest star in the room anymore, but that only added to my allure. A little age, a little polish—experience, darling. That's what sets me apart.

These days they approach with careful hands, lifting me from my resting spot. Their murmurs are reverent. I don't hear the exact words, but I don't need to. I know what I mean to them. They hoist me upward, securing me safely in position. And then I wait. Patiently. I always wait. Reminiscing.

Ah, what a life I've lived! Bright lights, spinning scenes, and crowds of adoring fans. Even now, as I rest in the quiet space, I can still hear the music of my younger days. The bass thumping through the floor, the high notes sparkling like champagne bubbles—those were my nights. I was the centre of attention, the one who made the room come alive.

INANIMATE CONFESSIONS

I can feel tonight stirring around me, the familiar buzz of preparation. It's been a while, but I know the signs. Chairs being pushed aside, laughter drifting in from the next room. Someone hums a tune, off-key but enthusiastic. Oh, it's happening. Tonight, I'll take my rightful place once again.

The chatter grows louder, the hum of life gathering momentum. The room is small—a far cry from the grandeur I've known—but it pulses with promise. The faint scent of cologne mingles with the unmistakable warmth of bodies drawn together by celebration. I feel their excitement like static in the air.

It's not the grand ballrooms of my heyday—no parquet floors or sweeping gowns here. But it's cozy, alive with the energy of friends gathering to celebrate. A record spins on an old turntable, and I recognise the tune. Oh, yes, this one's a classic. They have taste.

Then, it happens.

The first beam of light finds me, tentative at first, like a brushstroke on a blank canvas. I burst into life, scattering fragments of brilliance across the walls, the ceiling, their faces. Gasps echo softly, and I can feel their awe. They've remembered. It's always like this—the way they fall silent for a beat, the moment they let themselves surrender to the atmosphere I create.

The music swells, and I begin to move. Slowly at first, a gentle sway, gathering momentum as the bassline takes over. The room responds, bodies swaying, hands reaching. Laughter bubbles up, a melody all its own. The hours blur together in a tapestry of sound and movement. I spin faster, scattering light like fireworks, painting the room in gold and silver. They're in my world now.

But it doesn't last forever. It never does.

But no matter. I've been around long enough to know how these things go. My moment in the spotlight may be fleeting, but it's mine, and I'll cherish it. After all, not everyone gets to be the life of the party.

The music slows, the tempo softens, and so do I. My spin becomes a languid sway, matching the mood as couples pair off, leaning into each other under the dimming light. The chatter quiets, replaced by the murmurs of tired voices and the shuffle of feet reluctant to leave. The night is ending, and with it, my moment.

They lower me carefully, as they always do, their hands gentle but distracted. I can feel their energy dissipating, their thoughts drifting elsewhere. They wrap me up, my surface still warm from the lights, and place me back in my corner. The world outside grows quieter as the party disperses. The room empties, the echoes fading into stillness.

And then, silence.

It's not the first time I've been put away, and it won't be the last. I've learned to be patient, to treasure the moments when I'm lifted into the light and the room dances to my brilliance. Until then, I'll wait here in the dark, my surface dull but my spirit undimmed.

After all, a Mirrorball doesn't just reflect light. It reflects life.

THE MIRRORBALL

The Performer

The air buzzed with anticipation, electric with excitement. I was ready, every fibre of my being focused on the moment ahead. The velvet curtain swayed slightly, the whispers of the audience behind it barely audible over the thundering pulse in my ears. I didn't need to see them to feel their presence—hundreds of expectant eyes waiting for magic to unfold.

The lights dimmed, and the world beyond the curtain hushed. My moment was here.

I moved into position, trembling with a mix of fear and exhilaration. The music began, a delicate piano melody building into a sweeping crescendo. I launched forward, carried by rhythm and instinct, each step precise, each movement purposeful. The stage was my world now, the spotlight my only companion.

As the melody swirled around me, I lost myself in the flow. Each leap felt like flying, each turn an assertion of control in a chaotic world. The audience couldn't see the strain, the effort it took to maintain such grace. They didn't see how I fought against the pull of gravity, how I endured the ache that spread with each moment. I didn't let them see.

This was my purpose, my art. And art demanded sacrifice.

I pushed harder as the music swelled, spinning faster, leaping higher. The applause came in waves, crashing over me, but I didn't slow. Not yet. The performance wasn't finished. My role wasn't complete.

And then came the moment of truth, the final sequence. The music surged, and I flung myself into it with everything I had left. The movements were perfect, fluid and strong. But I could feel it—a small, imperceptible shift. A weakness growing. My body begged for rest, but I denied it. Not now. Not yet.

The last note rang out, and the stage plunged into silence. For a heartbeat, the world stood still. Then the applause erupted, a thunderous roar that seemed to shake the floor beneath me. I stood tall, soaking in their adoration, my heart swelling with pride.

But pride is fleeting on a ballet stage.

As the curtain fell, so did I. The adrenaline ebbed, leaving only the searing ache of overexertion. I was carried away, my role complete, and set aside as the celebration continued without me. The others moved on, their focus shifting to the next act, the next spectacle.

I waited, alone in the quiet, my body aching and worn. I remembered the cheers, the praise. I tried to hold onto the feeling of being vital, of being needed. But deep down, I knew the truth. Tomorrow, someone else would take my place. Their movements would be lighter, fresher. They wouldn't carry the wear of a hundred performances.

The door opened, and she appeared—the one I had shared the stage with. Her face was flushed with triumph, her expression radiant. She reached for me, holding me briefly, almost tenderly. But her eyes betrayed her thoughts. She was assessing the damage, deciding whether I could endure another show.

A sigh. And then, she carried me to a dim corner of the room, placing me gently but decisively into the shadows. I wanted to believe she would come back for me, that I hadn't reached the end. But her footsteps faded, leaving me alone with the sound of muffled voices beyond the walls.

As the hours stretched into the night, I let go of the cheers, the lights, the fleeting joy of the stage. I had given everything, and for a moment, it had been enough. That moment was mine, forever etched into the grooves of my being.

Even if the curtain never rose for me again.

I lay motionless in the corner, satin frayed, toes worn bare—a silent testament to a performance well-lived.

THE POINTE SHOES

The Last Sip

He felt the warmth seep into his skin, a familiar heat that filled him from the inside out. The morning light poured in through the wide windows, brushing his skin with a soft glow. It was his favourite time of day. Everything was fresh, new, full of potential.

Across the table, she was distracted, one hand scrolling through her phone, the other reaching for him absently. He didn't mind. These moments were never about her undivided attention. It was enough to be part of her routine, to have a place in her life. When her fingers brushed his sides, he felt whole.

Her lips touched him gently. Each time seemed to rejuvenate her, chasing the fog from her eyes and replacing it with clarity. He liked to think he made her day better, that he was more than just a habit. There was comfort between them, wasn't there? Maybe even love? He felt her tension ease as his company soothed her.

The minutes ticked by, the morning slipping through their shared silence. He watched her, the way she furrowed her brow at an email, the absent smile that touched her lips when a message popped up on her screen. He'd been here for so many mornings, seen so many versions of her—rushed, contemplative, even teary-eyed on occasion. He'd been there for all of it.

But today felt different.

He noticed it in the way she held him, her touch lighter than usual, her movements slower. There was an air of finality in the way she lingered with him, as if savouring something fleeting. He tried to ignore the pang in his chest, the creeping sense that this morning might not end the way others did.

The warmth inside him dwindled, fading with each passing second. He wanted to hold onto it, to stretch these moments out just a little longer. But there was no stopping the inevitable. He could feel her shifting, her attention already elsewhere. Her phone buzzed again, and she removed her hand from him without a glance.

The emptiness spread through him, a hollow ache that he knew all too well. He watched as she rose from the table, grabbing her bag and coat in a hurried flurry. She didn't look back, didn't even spare him a second thought as she rushed out the door.

For a while, he sat there in the quiet, staring at the crumbs she'd left on the table. The warmth was gone now, his insides cool and barren. He thought about all the mornings they'd shared, the countless times he'd been there for her without fail. He'd always been ready, always full of warmth for her. Wasn't that enough?

The sound of footsteps broke the silence. Someone entered the kitchen—a different set of hands, larger, clumsier. They grabbed him without care, tilting him roughly over the sink. He felt the last remnants of himself spill out, a brief, bitter farewell to the role he'd played.

Then came the worst part. Dunking him into lukewarm soapy water and shaking him around. Not even the dignity of a proper wash from this guy!

He thought about her, about the warmth they'd shared, about the small but vital role he'd played in her morning. It was fleeting, but it had meant something. At least, it had to him.

Alas, the world went on without him, the hum of life continuing. But he'd been there. And for a little while, he'd mattered. Tomorrow? Same. Unless she chooses tea.

THE COFFEE CUP

The Morning Jolt

I know what I look like, okay? I'm not sleek, not flashy. You won't find me on the cover of some glossy magazine, and that's fine. I'm not here for glamour. I'm here to *work*.

Every morning, without fail, I'm called upon to perform my magic. The ritual is always the same: a sleepy shuffle into the room, a grunted greeting, and then—*the press*. Oh, how I live for that moment! The soft click, the slow build of warmth, the hum of energy coursing through me.

They rely on me, you know. They don't say it outright, but I can tell. Without me, their day doesn't start. I bring the heat, the focus, the clarity. I turn those groggy eyes into sharp, determined stares.

But do I get a thank you? A word of appreciation for my tireless efforts? Never. They don't even clean me properly, just a quick swipe across the visible areas and then back to my lonely corner until they need me again. I'm not bitter, though. Well, maybe just a little.

Still, I know my worth. I may not be the star of the show, but I'm the one who makes it all possible. And that's enough for me.

THE HUMBLE TOASTER

The Watcher

I've always been here for her, standing quietly in the background, ready when she needs me. Every morning, she comes to me, her movements slow and unguarded, her face soft with the remnants of sleep. I watch as she rubs her eyes, muttering something under her breath about how early it feels. She never sees me roll my eyes in response, but it's a familiar ritual, one I've grown to love.

She stands before me with a furrowed brow, brushing her hair into something resembling order. She's always critical of herself at first, always muttering about stray hairs or dark circles. I don't reach out, take her hand, and tell her she's beautiful just as she is. Instead, I give her space, allowing her to see herself clearly. It's the best I can do, and some days, that's enough.

I've seen her in every mood. The mornings when she's radiant with excitement, bouncing on the balls of her feet as she picks out a dress for a special occasion. The evenings when she's exhausted, wiping away the day with tired hands. The quiet nights when she lingers, examining herself with a vulnerability she rarely shows to anyone else.

She doesn't always realise how far she's come, but I do. When we first met, she was younger, unsure of herself. She would glance up only briefly, her shoulders hunched as if bracing for judgment. Over time, she started to lift her gaze for longer, hold herself up straighter. She learned to hold her own gaze, to see her reflection not as something to be fixed, but as something to be proud of.

I've seen her try on countless outfits, practicing her smile, spinning in circles like a little girl. She always tilts her head, searching for approval, and I give it freely. I've also seen the moments she'd rather forget—quiet tears, lips trembling, her fingers tracing invisible fault lines only she can see. Those are the hardest times. I can't change the way she feels, but I can hopefully reassure her that she's strong enough to face herself, even on the hardest days.

Tonight, she pauses in front of me, a quiet smile tugging at the corners of her lips. Her hair is pinned up neatly, and her eyes are framed by the faintest trace of eyeliner. She adjusts a necklace, turning her head to admire the way it catches the light. She looks happy. Confident.

"Not bad," she murmurs, her fingers brushing the fabric of her dress. I want to tell her she's stunning, that her light comes from within, but I stay silent. I can only watch as she walks away, the sound of her heels fading down the hall.

Later, she returns with a box tucked under one arm. Her hands are careful as she moves me, smoothing away marks that her fingers leave behind. I wonder if she's moving on, if this is the end of our time together. But instead, she carries me to another room, one with fresh paint on the walls and a bed that's just been made. She places me in the corner, adjusting my position until I catch the light just right.

She steps back, tilts her head, and smiles at me.

"Perfect," she says softly, before walking away.

And there I am, a mirror in a new room, my frame gleaming in the evening light. I wait patiently, ready to reflect her strength and beauty again tomorrow.

THE BEDROOM MIRROR

A Safe Space

She had a way of making them feel seen, even in their quietest moments. She never demanded attention, never needed to be the centre of things. She just *was*, quietly observing, offering her presence when it was needed most. Her role was simple, but it carried meaning—especially for those who truly understood what it was to lean on her.

At first, they came in weary, their eyes wide with the exhaustion of long travels. Some of them were too tired to even speak, dragging their bags through the door and straight to the corner. She would always be there, waiting, ready to support them.

She didn't expect them to know her immediately, didn't mind when they hesitated before sitting. There were always moments of uncertainty in the beginning, a cautiousness that came with being in an unfamiliar space. But eventually, they would settle into her warmth, her familiarity. They would relax.

Some were light-hearted, their laughter filling the room as they swapped stories of distant places and adventures. She held their excitement with ease while they told their tales, offering them a place to rest their tired bodies and, in the process, letting them rest their souls as well. She was a patient listener, absorbing the energy around her, and always offering just the right amount of space to allow them to open up.

Others came quieter. She could feel the weight of their days pressing on them, the heaviness of unspoken thoughts. Their shoulders were slumped, their eyes tired, and though they would smile politely, there was a distant sadness to them. She never judged. She just accepted them, letting them open up to her when they finally felt comfortable enough. The world could be a tough place, she knew that well, but she could offer a little solace in her soft embrace.

She didn't have many words of her own. She didn't need to. Her role was simple: to hold, to offer comfort, to give the space for people to feel safe. In their company, she felt a quiet satisfaction. There was no rush. No expectation. It was enough to be there, to offer a place for them to rest, whether for a few minutes or a few hours.

Her days were marked by change—constant comings and goings. Some people would stay for a long while, filling the space with their presence. Others came and went quickly, their visits brief but meaningful. Each of them left something behind, whether it was a shared laugh, a quiet conversation, or simply the weight of their body resting gently against her.

She was there through the early mornings, when they'd linger over breakfast, laughing or nursing their cups of tea. She was there when they'd retreat in the evening, tired from the day's adventures, curling up in the warmth of her space as they flipped through books or chatted with newfound friends.

She saw them at their best, when they were full of energy and hope, eager to see the world. She saw them at their lowest, when they would come to her for solace, their hearts heavy with the weight of homesickness or disappointment. She never turned anyone away, never asked for anything in return. She simply held them, as best as she could.

In the stillness of the night, when the noise of the hostel had faded, she was there, patiently waiting. The soft rustle of the sheets in the next room was the only sound she could hear, but she knew, somehow, that tomorrow would bring more people, more moments. They would come to her, seeking comfort or simply a place to pause in their journey.

Eventually, the door would open again, and another soul would wander in. She would be ready for them. They'd sit, relax, talk, or stay silent, but they would always be received with the same quiet support. She had no grand ambitions, no dreams beyond being there for the ones who needed her.

But she knew—just as she always had—that her job was important, even if it was often overlooked.

She wasn't flashy, not glamorous. But that didn't matter.

She was a steady presence in this space, always there when people needed her most. And for all the wear and tear, the crumbs and spills, the marks left by countless bodies, she didn't mind. She was here to hold them for as long as they needed, without asking anything in return.

This couch had seen so much, yet never complained. She just waited, enduring, ever patient, ever ready.

THE BACKPACKERS' COUCH

Companion

He remembered the first time he'd left. It was with nothing but the essentials—just a few clothes, a toothbrush, and the kind of naïve optimism that only someone with no experience can truly have. He didn't need anything more. The world was wide, and he was ready to take it on, one step at a time. His skin felt fresh, his movements smooth, his body light, like he could go anywhere, be anywhere. He had barely any weight to carry. Freedom.

She didn't pack much either. A jacket, some trousers and shorts, a few shirts. There wasn't much to her, but there was something in her eyes- the kind of spark you can't fake. She was ready for the road, for whatever might come next. He was more than just a companion; He was the key to her escape. A trusted friend.

The first few weeks were full of adventure. They were both new to this. She led him through cities he'd never seen, over mountains that seemed endless, through rainstorms that soaked them to the bone. And all the while, he felt the weight of new experiences stacking up. A souvenir here, a new jacket there. A book she picked up along the way, a blanket bought from a street vendor. She'd add something and he would bear it all, without complaint.

At first, it was just the essentials. But the longer they travelled, the more things piled up. Little by little, he began to feel heavy. A pair of shoes bought in a bustling market. A photograph, a memento of a night spent laughing with strangers who felt like friends. Trinkets, cards, maps, each piece a small marker of where they'd been. He could feel it all inside- the weight of their memories, the moments of joy, the occasional pang of homesickness.

He didn't mind at first. Didn't mind at all. She was discovering the world, and he was a part of that. Every step, every journey, every new face. They were building something together, creating a life out of shared experiences. It felt right. It felt *good*.

But after a while, things started to change. The load, the weight of it all, became too much. He could feel her slowing down, the weight pulling her down with each step. The items they'd collected along the way, the souvenirs, the keepsakes- everything that once felt so important, now just felt heavy. He could hear her struggling, the frustration building. There were moments when she looked at him, her shoulders slumping, as though she wished we could just leave it all behind.

He didn't understand it at first. They had built this together, hadn't they? Each item he held was a piece of her journey. But as they walked through crowded streets, as they trekked through endless landscapes, he began to feel the frustration in the way she moved

And then, after a longer period of stillness than usual, where she'd had time to collect a few more 'things' and add a second bag to carry, she did what she needed to do.

They were in a small town, the kind of place they used to love, full of life, full of possibility. The kind of town that sells essentials to travellers, and the kind of town where you meet others easily.

She only did what was sensible and although it stung, he understood. She replaced him. She sold him to another traveller and packed everything into her newer, bigger backpack.

As he felt himself lifted again, he realised something. He wasn't meant to stay the same. He wasn't meant to remain a static thing, just a container of memories. He was meant to move, to change, to carry new journeys, new adventures. This was his purpose.

He was ready to face a new challenge and new adventures, with a new girl. Of course, she would soon discover that the beautiful and expensive ring her predecessor had bought in Nairobi was still hidden there in his side pocket.

But, one person's loss…

THE TRAVELLERS FIRST BACKPACK

Getting Dirty

I was born for this. The fresh smell of the earth, the soft crumble of dirt in my grasp. There's nothing better, nothing more thrilling than the promise of what's hiding just beneath the surface. And let me tell you, I've been digging for years.

The first time she took me outside, I knew I was meant to be hers. She crouched low, her fingers brushing the soil, and I could barely contain my excitement. The sun was warm on my back, and the air was alive with the scent of grass and dew. She gave me a purpose that day. "Come on," she said, and I didn't need to be told twice. I dove straight into the dirt, pushing aside clumps of earth with enthusiasm.

We spent what felt like hours out there, uncovering secrets buried beneath the surface. Tiny, wriggling worms, smooth stones that gleamed in the sunlight, and the occasional root that tried to stand in our way—I tackled them all. Every moment felt like a triumph.

She liked to have me nearby when she planted, although I wasn't always sure she appreciated me in those moments. Seeds, small and hopeful, tucked gently into the ground. I loved the way she admired her work, brushing the soil from her hands as if to say, "Just right".

As the seasons passed, I grew and gained confidence. Spring was always my favourite—soft dirt and the smell of rain. Summer was harder, the ground dry and stubborn, but I never gave up and neither did she. By autumn, we'd be clearing out the old, making way for the new. And winter? Winter was quiet, the garden asleep under frost, but I'd dream of the days we'd dig again.

But after every visit to the garden, she'd clean the dirt off me. Her hands were steady, reassuring. She always made sure I was ready for the next adventure.

I may not be as strong as I once was, or as shiny, but I'm still here. Still hers. And as long as there's earth to dig, I'll keep going.

I rest on the edge of the garden bed, handle worn and smooth, my metal flecked with rust. The soil beneath my blade is fresh and ready, a quiet testament to years of service- and to the joy of digging into life's little adventures.

THE GARDEN TROWEL

The Silent Witness

The room was quiet, bathed in the soft glow of the afternoon sun filtering through lace curtains. Dust motes floated lazily in the golden light, drifting over me and the books I held. The spines lined up against my body were my pride—stories of adventure, heartbreak, and discovery, each one chosen with care. I felt stronger carrying them, a silent guardian of stories and secrets.

Life in this household was predictable. The mornings brought the smell of fresh coffee and the gentle hum of a radio. Afternoons were a lull of quiet productivity, punctuated by soft footsteps or the occasional creak of the floorboards. And evenings were alive with the sound of laughter, conversations, or the tapping of fingers on a keyboard. I knew this rhythm well. It had become my comfort.

But tonight, the air was different.

Their voices started low, simmering with irritation. At first, I thought it was a passing disagreement, one of those fleeting moments that quickly gave way to laughter or apologies. But the volume rose, and the tension in the air thickened. I braced myself as the argument escalated, ricocheting off the walls like a relentless storm.

"Why aren't you listening to me?!" her voice rang out, sharp and wounded.

"Maybe if you said something worth listening to!" he shot back, his words like a whip.

I felt the vibrations of their anger ripple through the room. The sound shook me to my core—every word a blow I could not deflect. I wanted to stop it, to shout over their voices, to make them see reason. But I couldn't. I could only stand there, holding my books, hoping it would end soon.

The fight became a tempest. She gestured wildly, knocking over a vase. The crash made me flinch, though I stood firm. Water seeped into the rug, mixing with shattered ceramic, a scene of chaos reflected in the glass of the framed photos on the wall. He didn't move to clean it up. Instead, he stormed past me, the gust of his anger rustling the leaves of a potted plant nearby.

She collapsed onto the couch, her shoulders heaving with silent sobs. The room fell still, save for the uneven rhythm of her breathing. I wanted to comfort her somehow, to remind her of the stories she's enjoyed in the past- tales of resilience, of hope, of love found and fought for. But now was not the time to interrupt. I remained a mute observer of her frailty, knowing I couldn't help right now.

Time passed. Maybe hours. She eventually rose, her face a mask of exhaustion, and began to clean up the shattered vase. The water was gone, the shards swept into a dustpan, but the tension remained, like a stain that no amount of scrubbing could remove.

Days went by, and the house was quieter than usual. The argument hung in the air, an invisible spectre neither of them could exorcise. They spoke in clipped tones, avoiding eye contact, their movements around the room carefully choreographed to avoid crossing paths. The space between them grew, and I felt it in every creak of the floorboards.

One evening, as the sun dipped below the horizon and the room filled with shadows, he had clearly remembered me and my books and, although hesitant, he selected one from the collection. It was a novel about forgiveness, its spine worn from years of use. He sat down on the couch, flipping through the pages without really reading.

She entered a few moments later, a mug of tea in her hands. She paused, watching him, then set the mug on the coffee table. They didn't speak, but their silence felt different this time—softer, less jagged. She picked up her knitting, settling into the chair opposite him.

For a long while, the only sounds were the rustle of pages and the quiet clink of knitting needles. It wasn't a resolution, not yet, but it was a start.

As they sat there, I stood silently in my corner, holding their stories, their history. I had witnessed their anger and now their tentative steps toward reconciliation. I would continue to stand, steadfast, bearing witness to their lives.

That is my purpose, after all. I am just a bookshelf. But I hold worlds within me, and maybe, just maybe, those worlds can help to heal a few wounds.

THE BOOKSHELF

Tale as Old as Time

When she first arrived, I could feel the excitement in the air. It was palpable, almost electric. She held me in her hand, her grip tight with anticipation as she stepped over the threshold for the first time. The door clicked open, and I could feel the rush of her breath, the hope in her eyes as she stepped into her new life.

The house was quiet then, still, as though it was waiting too. The walls awaited fresh paint, the floors a little tatty but ready for a makeover. There was a soft, almost reverent silence as she moved around, touching things, adjusting little details that made the place feel hers. The curtains were drawn back to let in the light, and for the first time, the space felt full of potential. It wasn't just four walls and a roof—it was the first thing she'd ever truly owned!

She didn't say it outright, of course. But I could sense it. The pride. The joy. This was her accomplishment. This house was *hers*, and she was already imagining the beautiful spaces she'd create within it. I'd been there for every step, easing open the door to let her inside, watching as she made her mark, transforming the empty rooms into something more.

But as the weeks turned to months, I felt something change. The initial excitement faded, and the weight of ownership began to settle in. The bills piled up—electricity, gas, council tax—things that hadn't crossed her mind when she was signing the papers. The house that once felt full of possibilities started to feel heavy. I could feel the tension in her shoulders as she fumbled at the door. She would glance at the stack of letters on the table, her face drawn, before turning away and getting on with things.

The house, for all its charm, started to become a burden. The creak of the floors at night, the leaks in the roof, the pipes that sometimes groaned in protest. And every repair seemed to come at a cost. Every task she ticked off the list was met with a new one. She started to leave the door ajar when she got home, a slight sign of impatience, as though it was just another thing she had to do, another small annoyance in her day. But really it was often because she didn't plan to be there for long. In, do the necessary, then leave, try not to look at all of the unfinished work that would cost more to complete. Try not to be here long enough to hear the neighbours slamming doors and watch the walls shake between the two houses.

Now, she hesitated before unlocking the door. The same excitement that once accompanied her arrival seemed replaced by a tired reluctance. The house had become just a place to sleep, a thing she needed to manage rather than enjoy. I had always been the one to let her in, but now it felt like I was the last part of her day she had to contend with before retreating into the silence of her own thoughts.

It's been like this for a few years now.

But now, somehow, something is shifting again. Slowly, almost imperceptibly at first. She started to tend to the little things— repainting a door, fixing a broken window latch, arranging a vase of flowers on the table. The cracks in the walls seemed a little less significant when she saw the way the sunlight caught the table, or when she sank into the couch at the end of the day and realised how much she loved the way it all looked together.

The joy returned, not in grand gestures, but in the small moments. A quiet cup of tea on a Sunday afternoon, the way the house felt warm when the heating clicked on. The clutter that once seemed overwhelming started to feel like the collection of memories that had built up over time. Slowly, she began to see it not just as a house, but as her *home* again.

And I? I was there, still opening the door. Every time she walked through it, there was a softness in her steps, a little more peace in her heart.

She didn't need to say anything. I could feel it in the way she would leave more slowly, taking more care, as if holding onto the feeling a little longer before she closed the door behind her. There was no hesitation on arrival anymore. There was no regret. She had made peace with it, with the imperfections of the house, and with her place within it.

It was hers. Not just the structure. Not just the bricks and mortar. But the love she put into it, the care she showed, and the way she started to call it *home*.

There were others like me, in various drawers here and there, but I was the one always right here, at the threshold. I still fit smoothly into the lock, turning without a second thought, ready to welcome her back into the place she worked so hard to make her own.

THE GREEN HOUSEKEY

Dust in the Light (Part 2)

It was that moment, that single moment, that had always felt so far out of reach. The kind of thing you only daydream about, the way you dream about getting up in the middle of a night, and suddenly you can speak your mind, your voice carrying in the air. Finally. Finally!

She's here. I can feel her presence, even before I see her face. The light- it's different this time. It's not just a beam cutting through the space, catching the dust in its dance. This time, it fills the room, illuminating everything around me. The shadows are scattered, chased away by a warmth I've almost forgotten, a kind of golden brightness I had convinced myself was a myth.

And then, there she is. Her silhouette, the way the light catches her hair, the way she breathes in sharply as she sees me. I can feel her excitement. Her fingers- those familiar hands, trembling ever so slightly- brush against the other things before they reach me.

I've been here for so long, in this dark, forgotten place. But, now that she sees me, I can't help but feel a thrill, a rush of recognition. I'm *needed* again. *Finally.*

There's no grand ceremony. There's no fanfare or applause. It's just a hand, with a quiet steadiness, lifting me from the shadows. It feels unreal, as if I could blink and I'd be back in that forsaken corner, gathering dust once again. But no- she doesn't let me go. She doesn't put me down. Instead, I look up, and I see her face, satisfied, silent, absorbing this moment of reunion.

She found me. She's here. She's ready to go.

It's not until she smiles, not until I see that look of recognition that I realise- she *did* know all along. She never forgot about me, even though it seemed like I had vanished, lost in the dark for so long. It wasn't that she didn't need me; it was just... life got in the way.

But now? Now I am the key to her next journey. The only thing standing between her and the next adventure.

She flips me open with a quick flick of her fingers, her eyes scanning the pages with a kind of reverence, as if to check that everything is still there, intact. I've waited so long to feel that gentle turn of the pages, the familiar memories in the air – the travel, the stamps, the new places, the new people. This is what I was made for.

We're going to places I've never seen, and I'm going to be there for it all. I can feel her energy, her eagerness, and with it, the realisation that we're both leaving something behind. But we're also stepping into something new. Something thrilling.

The drawer that once held me so tightly is fae from empty. Those old letters and receipts may never see the light of day again, but that isn't going to be *my* fate anymore.

THE REDISCOVERED PASSPORT

ABOUT THE AUTHOR

K. M. Wicks spent the years from 2013-2017 travelling and gathering stories from misspent and well-spent days, which were published into a blog under the name of The Troublesome Traveller.

In the quieter years following her travels, she rediscovered some of her unpublished stories and was reminded of the joy she'd felt creating them. Once reminded of a more carefree and whimsical time, she vowed never to lose sight her story-telling soul again, and this book marks the first of many.

Now, she will endeavor to revisit and republish those previously unshared stories for others to enjoy.

Printed in Great Britain
by Amazon